The Illusory
STEP-BALL -CHANGE

Published in the UK in 2021 by EnPointe Publishing

Paperback ISBN 978-1-7399882-2-7
    eBook ISBN 978-1-7399882-1-0

Typeset by SpiffingCovers

The Illusory
STEP-BALL -CHANGE

LillySan

"If your illusions are shattered, it means you are getting closer to reality."

SADHGURU

CHAPTER 1

Curtains Up

Lizzie settled into the plush airplane seat after fumbling with the seat belt. The engines of the Boeing 747 started up with a huge roar, like a lion waking up from its slumber. After what seemed like eternity, the plane finally began to taxi slowly down the long runway. Lizzie's stomach felt as though it was tied up in knots as the plane started its ascent into the sky. The excitement of being in an airport and flying for the first time took her thoughts momentarily away from last night's tears, from the breakup of the first love in her life. As the plane began to glide smoothly and the excitement started to ebb, her mind goes back to the breakup. Thoughts flitted through her mind as she searched for what she had done wrong. She could not stop questioning in her mind why her boyfriend had been so nasty to her, and why he no longer wanted to be with her. Whenever they were together, she felt happy and safe. Lizzie had never been with any man before he came into her life. Suave and mature, he taught her so much and opened her eyes to the wonders of intimate sexual pleasures. Lizzie wrung her hands in distress and thought to herself:

"Was it because I said I would love to have his baby?"

Tears stung her eyes; it was only a flippant remark she had made on their last weekend getaway. Surely he wouldn't have taken it seriously? Finding no answers to the questions that raced through her mind, Lizzie forced herself to lock her emotions away and not dwell on her heartache. She closed her eyes and pinched herself. She could not believe she is flying to Mexico after securing her equity contract.

Memories came flooding back of her very first day at Miss Jean's dance school. It made her laugh to recall that she had no dancing shoes, no money to pay for classes, but somehow or other, Miss Jean allowed her to join the class once a week. The dance classes were the only time and place where she could escape from the bullies in the school and the predators at home. Lizzie smiled thinking back to her school friend Sharon, who had told her about a local dancing school where anyone could join. As far as she could remember, she had always loved dancing. She flinched as she remembered the ugly scene with her mum when she announced to her that she wanted to go to a dancing school. Her mum said no, using the excuse that she was only nine years old and that there was no one to take her there. She had no idea where she got her courage, but Lizzie ignored her Mum's refusal to allow her to go, making a plan to go on her own. The next morning after that conversation with her mum, she quietly slipped out of the front door and headed for what she knew was a short cut to the hall where the dancing classes were held. Even though Lizzie knew she should not go down the back alley to get to the hall, she still did so because she was running late. She darted through the alley without looking back, running all the way to Miss Jean's dance school. She came out of the alley into a T-junction, manoeuvred herself around the metal gate and walked into the entrance of the dancing hall. She heard the piano playing; the music sounded alien to her ears, and she hovered uncertainly by the door. In the far corner, she saw two mothers, one of whom is very fat and Mediterranean-looking. She had beautiful long black hair tied back neatly at the back of her head. She was fussing over a little girl, making sure that she had her tights on and tying the ribbons in her ballet shoes. Lizzie saw another girl sat next to the other mother who was dressed more like Lizzie's own Mum, button-down shirt with a thick V-neck sweater over it, bright happy pants and opaque tights. The little girl had long legs and a beautifully sweet face. Lizzie stared at her, mesmerised. Then she heard a loud voice:

"Come on in!"

For a moment, Lizzie froze. She was not sure what to do. Then tentatively, she stepped into the hall. A lady in a mid-length skirt was seated at a table, legs astride, wearing slouch socks with leather court shoes on her feet, which looked too small for her as the top of her feet was bulging out of them. As Lizzie lifted her gaze, she saw the rest of Miss Jean – a very buxom lady with breasts that look like they are about to pop out of her tight blouse, sitting with arms crossed in front of her. A small tin box sat on the table. Sitting next to her was a nice-looking young lady holding a pen and a register. Lizzie approached the table stealthily. Miss Jean gave Lizzie a huge smile and asked her what she wanted. Lizzie pulled her shoulders back to make herself appear taller and said assertively that she wanted to come for dancing lessons. Miss Jean paused, lowered her glasses and stared fiercely at Lizzie. Lizzie shrunk a little with fear under that intense gaze. Her lips started to quiver, and she could feel her eyes starting to water; her aspiration of wanting to be a dancer began to slip away as Miss Jean's eyes bored into hers. In an abrupt tone, Miss Jean said:

"Okay, have you got money?"

In a small voice, Lizzie replied:

"No, I don't have any money"

Miss Jean looked at her fixedly for a while, then she said:

"Go take your shoes and socks off and join the other girls."

From that moment on, Miss Jean's dancing school became Lizzie's haven — a happy, nurturing place where she could fantasize about a make-believe world of music and dance. One night a week, she would have friends to talk to and felt that she belonged. It was a sanctuary where her confidence was slowly built. Her mum never once came to watch her dance. Miss Jean gave her a scholarship if she promised to turn up every week. Eventually, through baby-sitting jobs, Lizzie bought her first pair of dancing shoes. She was so pleased that she no longer had to accept the hand-me-downs from the other mums. She finally had her own pair of dancing shoes. Lizzie's time at Miss Jean's gave her the confidence to build her dreams of becoming a professional dancer. Who would have thought that a small rundown community hall hired by Miss Jean, whose generosity and concealed kindness kept a little girl's dreams alive?

Coming back to the present, Lizzie could hardly believe she had landed this amazing seven-month equity contract which is going to bring her dreams as a professional dancer to reality. She is going to become famous, she thought. She pinched herself again to check if this is all a dream. But no, she was on a Boeing 747 airplane to Houston, Texas and then on to Mexico City from there. She could hear, just in front of her, behind the curtains, an air stewardess talking to a passenger. She was enthralled by the air stewardess' soft cooing voice.

"What would you like sir? We have wine, soft drinks, juices."

Lizzie listened intently to the conversation that was going on behind the curtain. She got excited, sitting up in her seat in anticipation of the amazing service that she would soon receive. She saw the shiny high heel shoes of the air stewardess peeping through the curtains. With a swish they were pushed across. Lizzie had never seen such an immaculately dressed woman before – deep red lips, long painted nails, standing tall in her high heel shoes. Her starched, pristine uniform silhouettes her skinny frame. She stood in front of Lizzie and in a coarse voice, a complete turnaround from the earlier soft voice, announced that lunch was either a meat or vegetarian dish and there would be tea and coffee. The air stewardess stood poised with a pen and a pad, ticking off the list of what the people in her aisle wanted. At that point, Lizzie realized that class and money mattered, even in an airplane.

Lizzie, brought up to be always polite and respectful, said "please and thank you." She thought to herself:

"You could have been nicer to us."

But Lizzie did not hold it against the air stewardess, knowing full well that she was just doing her job. At a second glance, Lizzie realized that underneath all that thick make-up she wore, she was not young. Her glamourous flying days would soon be over. Unfortunately, on this flight, she just wasn't lucky enough to work solely in first class.

After finishing her rather dry and bland meal and her cup of watery tea, she settled into her seat for the ten hours thirteen minutes' flight. She closed her eyes and tried to go to sleep, but she was too excited to sleep. Her mind drifted back to the moment she had received a letter inviting her to audition for a famous theatre school. She could not believe that she had been picked as she had only mailed a polaroid photograph of herself in a jazz dance pose in front of her mum's 1970s wallpaper. Thinking back on the audition, she laughed to herself, remembering how stupid and naïve she had been. She simply had no idea of the expectation or how she should have prepared herself for the audition. Never having been to Central London before and being only sixteen at that time, she somehow managed to arrive on her own in plenty of time for the audition.

Lizzie was greeted by an elegantly-dressed lady who spoke in soft tones. She instructed Lizzie to get ready for the first part of the day. Lizzie had no idea what she was talking about. Seeing her confusion, the lady pointed Lizzie to a door. When she entered the room, there was a bevy of excited young girls with their mothers, getting changed for what was to be the ballet class. They all had black leotards, pink tights, pink ballet shoes with ribbons and had their hair up in a neat little bun. Lizzie started to well up inside, she did not know what to do. All she had was her emerald green leotard and a pair of black tights and her black ballet shoes and red jazz shoes, for which she had saved up for 6 weeks to buy. Feeling dejected, she went back outside to leave. The kind lady approached her and asked where she was going.

Lizzie said: "I don't have proper ballet clothes."

The lady with the lovely smile said: "Oh never mind, darling. You'll be fine. You should still go and audition."

Lizzie went back into the changing room and just managed to enter the studio in time for the ballet class. All the other girls stared at her sneeringly, as Lizzie obviously did not belong in this class.

Just like Miss Jean's dancing school, there was a table at the front, and sat there were three smartly-dressed people – two mature women and a younger man – they each had a notepad in front of them. Lizzy glanced at them, she could see that the younger man gave her an encouraging smile, as if to reassure her that it was okay. Lizzie thought of Miss Jean. She pulled herself up straight, and once the music began, she just went into her fantasy world of dancing. Coming to life with a big smile on her face, Lizzie danced her way through the audition without a care in the world.

At the end of the ballet class, they were told to get changed for the jazz dance audition and their solo dances. Lizzie didn't need to get changed, except to put on her red jazz shoes. She went to get a drink and came back and waited in the studio. In turn, all the dancers showed off their solo dances. Lizzie performed hers and was quietly proud of her performance. They then moved on to the jazz dance, and Lizzie was in her element. They were taught a short routine by the younger male teacher and Lizzie simply lapped it up as jazz was her forte.

"Thank goodness for Miss Jean's persistence in making sure that I accomplish a perfect step-ball-change."

After dancing the number several times, they were told the audition was nearly finished. The dancers were instructed to go and stand by the ballet barres again. Lizzie was feeling elated; she felt that she had performed better than she thought she would. It must have been her red jazz shoes that helped her. She knew in her heart that this was where she wants to be. This was her dream, and when she danced, all her problems and all her fears would melt away. Lizzie awaited her turn at the bar, the lady who sat in the middle got up and walked around. She went up to each dancer and asked each to do a développé. When it was Lizzie's turn, her right leg went up 90 degrees, the teacher forced it a bit higher. When she turned to do her left leg, she thought that she had done it just as high, but the teacher turned around to the others and said contemptuously:

"This hip is stiff!"

Lizzie felt tears rolling down her cheek as she woke up, she wiped them from her eyes. The memory of the rejection letter came back to her. It said:

"Your audition has not been successful due to a physical defect that would hinder training."

Lizzie thought that if only she had had the opportunity to see an osteopath or a physiotherapist to solve the problem, or that if she had parents who were more supportive, things would perhaps have turned out differently. Pinching herself again, she still could not believe that she finally had an equity contract and was closer to living her dreams.

Lizzie's thoughts were interrupted by an announcement on the plane. The airplane is about to land in Houston.

"This is the pilot speaking. Due to the bad weather, traffic control has requested that we remain in the air for a little while. Do not worry, we will get you safely to your destination."

But before he could finish speaking, there was a huge jolt, and the plane started to descend with speed, and then almost in the same breath, the plane started to tilt upward sharply. Many passengers on the plane gasped out loud, and some of the girls started to scream,

"We are going to die!"

Lizzie saw through the window the flashes of lightning above the cloud, and felt the plane shaking from side to side as it tried to navigate through the turbulence. Lizzie turned her head around and looked down the aisle. Two seats along, she saw Karen, one of the girls in the group, crying. Karen's ears were in excruciating pain. The air stewardess told her brusquely to shut up, but Karen was inconsolable. Lizzie passed some of her boiled sweets to Karen to suck on. From that moment, they became firm friends, like bees in a honey pot and inseparable.

Finally, with a huge bump, the airplane landed in Houston, Texas.

Lizzie was overwhelmed by her surroundings as everyone on the plane scrambled to get out. Her new friend Karen was still in a terrible state, the excruciating pain in her ears bringing tears to her eyes. Lizzie dragged Karen along. They cleared passport control surprisingly quickly and arrived at the Customs, meeting up with the other five girls who were standing in a long queue. Lizzie craned her neck to see if she could see the start of the line. She saw quite a number of security officers, and was surprised to see how many women there were, some of whom were pretty heavy-set and wearing visible firearms. Lizzie was rather taken aback at their brusque manner when they spoke to the passengers. She started to worry, trying to think if she had packed anything that might be seen as illegal. A thought rose in her head:

"Did I pack too many tampons? Are they going to stop me for that?"

She walked briskly with the other girls through the "Nothing to declare channel", breathing a huge sigh of relief when nobody stopped them. One of the girls, Elen, with

Mediterranean features but in fact she was really Welsh, went instead to the "Declare channel". She was stopped by an aggressive-looking female custom officer with thick glasses that enhanced her stern face.

"Open your case!" barked the customs officer.

Elen opened her case. The officer searched through it and found nothing but clothes, toiletries, and an apple. Lizzie saw the officer speaking to Elen as she pointed toward them. A male customs officer then started to approach. He asked all the other girls to follow him and herded them into a room. He started to go through everyone's cases and started to throw everything out. Lizzie was petrified as her thoughts returned to the seven months' supply of tampons in her case. She had no idea that she must declare them. Everything was strewn all over the counter. Luckily for Lizzie, the search stopped before they could find her tampons. Satisfied that there were no contrabands in any of the girls' cases, the officer finally waved his hand and said:

"You can go."

The girls made a rushed attempt to repack all their suitcases and dashed for their connecting flight to Mexico City, almost missing it. With no time to spare except for a quick visit to the toilet, Lizzie and the girls boarded their connecting flight. After that incident, each time they would go through customs, the girls would tease Elen and ask if she has any apples in her suitcase.

Finally, they scrambled on to the connecting flight. The plane was small, and all the other passengers on it were Mexicans. Not only that, there were also a few chickens and other livestock crammed into small cages. After an initial splutter, the propellers whirred noisily, and the flight took off dramatically with a huge roar. The storm that raged when they were landing earlier had not quite abated. Turbulence rocked the plane, as though some mad, invisible giant was shaking it like a toy: the chickens fluttered frantically in their cages, suitcases were falling off from the luggage compartment, babies were crying, and Karen, this time sitting next to Lizzie, started to whimper. Terrified, Lizzie was glad she managed to get to the toilet before boarding.

Lizzie thought to herself: "What a difference it is from the flight in the huge and glamorous Boeing 747."

Staring at the lightning flashes outside her small cabin window, Lizzie prayed quietly that the plane was not going to go down.

After all that turmoil, the plane landed very abruptly, wheels bouncing on the tarmac. Karen was crying again, whimpering so that her eardrums felt like they were about to burst. Although this was a sign, Lizzie was unaware that the next seven months were about to get even more dramatic.

The girls emerged from the plane just as the dusk light began to fall. The thunderstorm had stopped but the air was heavy and humid. Walking across the runway, the girls followed the other passengers to a small building. As they approached, Lizzie thought to herself:

"Surely this is not Mexico City? How could this be an international airport?"

As they entered the rather drab concrete building, a small and dusty sign said: "Welcome to Cancun."

This time, all the girls breezed through the customs checks, as the customs officers lazily waved everyone through. Waiting for them in the small, noisy and crowded arrival hall was a man wearing a cap, sunglasses and holding up a sign that says, "Cirque Magical". Dragging their suitcases, the girls followed him to a small van. With all the suitcases and the girls packed in like sardines, the van drove away from the airport down a dusty strip of road. Lizzie could see the sea and mangrove swamps on her side of the van. On the other side are many half-built high-rise buildings. The girls sat up with excitement when they saw the fancy-looking Playa Blanca hotel in view. But the van just sped on until it turned into a side street and stopped outside a drab motel. The girls disembarked with all their belongings and the man sped off, the wheels of his van screeching. The girls were very confused. It did not help that the hotel receptionist did not speak a word of English. Amidst the chaos and confusion, they somehow managed to get to their rooms, and Lizzie, exhausted from all that travelling, just fell asleep almost immediately without even unpacking.

The next day, around the breakfast table, Lizzie and the girls were all quiet and subdued. A man appeared before the girls and spoke in a thick Spanish accent:

"There's a change of plan. We are not going to Mexico City; we are going to join a sister circus in Chiquilá."

He told the girls they were leaving after breakfast. He reassured them that it was going to be okay, and that there was no need to worry as Equity knew about this. The girls looked at each other, saying nothing. Lizzie thought:

"This is rather odd!"

She felt her stomach constricting, like it always did when things don't feel right. But she said nothing to the girls.

After breakfast, the girls went back to their room, collected their suitcases, and went down to the reception area. A dusty old bus was waiting outside. It looked as if it was not going to make it to the end of the street, let alone a three-hour journey. The girls were herded into the bus and the long, bumpy ride began. As the bus passed through small and deserted villages, on roads that seem unpassable, Lizzie really started to worry, wondering where they were really going. When the girls tried to ask the driver, he did not seem to understand any English.

After repeated attempts to try and get him to understand they needed a toilet break, he finally stopped in a small garage where the girls were able to freshen up. The driver started to ramble in rapid Mexican and pointed animatedly to where the girls could buy some food and drink.

Finally, they arrived at their destination. Lizzie was dismayed to find that they were yet at another hotel which seemed deserted and rundown. The girls soon realized that they were the only guests staying there. The owner of the hotel came out to greet them and in halting English, told them to be ready for an 8am pick-up the next morning. Exhausted, the girls piled into their own rooms without having been offered an evening meal or any refreshments. Lizzie was glad that she did buy a bottle of water and some snacks when they had the toilet break, which she happily shared with Karen.

The next morning, without breakfast, the girls were picked up in the same old bus. Lizzie could see that they were leaving town. After 30 minutes' drive, the bus came to a halt by an open plot of land. In the distance was a huge tent with the name "Cirque Magical" blazoned over it. Lizzie realized, with a mixed feeling of dismay and bewilderment, that they were going to perform in a circus! She thought in disbelief:

"I have not attended all these training sessions at the ballet school to be bloody well performing in a circus tent in the middle of a muddy field. Why did I listen to the dance scout who encouraged me to audition for the tour? Damn Equity! What a fool I have been! I knew this Equity contract was too good to be true! Why didn't I stay teaching dance in Covent Garden?"

A loud voice cut through Lizzie's angry thoughts: "Come on darlings, this way!"

Lizzie turned around, and standing at the edge of the field was a young man with the blondest of hair sitting squarely over his face, skinny as a rake, hands on his hip, calling the girls over. She soon discovered his name is Jason, from Wokingham. He has been there for two months, Lizzie learned later. The girls piled into the tent behind Jason. They got to the back of the tent, climbed up some stairs and found themselves on the stage. There, waiting around, sitting, and chatting, was the rest of the company. Lizzie and the girls were greeted warmly by a rush of people and were bombarded by questions of how long they were going to be here, what had been happening back home in England, everyone talked excitedly over each other. Lizzie soon realized however that these people were excited not to see them, but that the new girls' arrival meant that they could soon go home. The new group had come to replace them.

Everyone else was still clucking like excited chickens. Suddenly, amidst the confusing chattering, a loud voice bellowed:

"QUIET!"

Everybody stopped talking. Lizzie saw, at the end of the stage, a big, burly man sat down on a chair. He had a crown of grey curly hair, like a lion's mane. Lizzie saw the silhouette of a young girl next to this man, softly stroking his mane of hair. She soon came to realize that the young girl's name is Maya, and she is the wife of Gustavo, the big burly man who owned the circus. They were told by him to come closer. The girls squeezed together at the front of the stage.

All of a sudden, there was a crisp and thunderous clap. Lizzie looked toward the centre aisle and she saw this figure walking toward the stage, as if he was a puppet. As he got closer, all Lizzie could think about was how this man looked like Parker from the Thunderbirds: sharp, pointed nose, bushy eyebrows that almost joined up with his sideburns, pursed lower lips. Lizzie stood there, staring, mouth almost wide-open. This spitting image of Aloysius Parker introduced himself as Roberto, the choreographer. Roberto has thick white hair, parted in the centre, sleekly swept back, highly likely zapped with plenty of hair spray to keep it in place. He wore an open-necked, bright green shirt, a wide lapel jacket and green flared trousers, a cigarette holder between his thin, yellow, and black-stained fingers. Lizzie thought to herself:

"I wonder what he's been using?"

Roberto walked over in a strangely rhythmical movement, his body wobbling like a person who has had too much to drink, not a strand of his swept-back white hair was out of place. His voice bellowed again like a turbo engine: 'Quiet!' At the back of the stage was a cage with lions. Even the lions stopped pacing. If anyone fell off the stage, they would literally lie on top of the lions' cage.

Gustavo introduced Lizzie and the new cast members, one at a time, to Roberto, as though they were meeting a king. Lizzie thought incredulously:

"What have I done? I have trained four years as a professional dancer, and here is this bird-like man standing in front of me, commanding me to turn around, do a demi-point, like Dr Coppelius' life-size dancing doll."

It was like a cattle market; all the girls were made to go through this rather humiliating "audition". Roberto's looks were so intense. It was as though his eyes were boring into hers, yet also not looking at her.

Finally, in a bored, monotonous tone as if he's said this numerous times, Roberto said in staccato Spanglish to the new cast members:

"You – not allowed to sunbathe, you – remain white, no burning your skin, no putting on weight. We need start promptly at 8.30 in the morning. We do two shows every night and four every Sunday."

With that, he turned and just left, trying to hasten his pace, but failing to walk in a straight line even though he was aided by his little boy assistant. Maya announced to the seven new cast members: "Stay for your costume fitting." The rest of the cast was then dismissed.

The girls were ushered to the back of the stage. Just to the left were some steps that led them down to a huge caravan. It was narrow and dark, with a low ceiling, rather like a gypsy caravan. On one side of the length of the trailer, glamourous costumes made of expensive satin, silk, fur and sparkling jewels were hung, crammed into each other, wall-to-wall. Above the rail was a shelf crammed full of different kinds of hats and headdresses. On the other side were twenty-one small, metal chairs, each dancer had a make-up space in front on the wall, with a small mirror and light bulbs all around. An incredulous thought flashed across Lizzie's mind:

"It feels like a cheap striptease joint. You can't even swing a cat in there, how are they going to fit 21 dancers in here?"

Lizzie stepped into the trailer and was shown her place by the dance captain, Maya. No sooner had she sat down in her place, still bewildered by the whole thing, the musty, still air enveloping her, when Maya flapped her arms, gesturing at Lizzie to follow her to the back of the stage. There was no proper changing facility, only some rather unglamorous bits of curtains were hung on three sides. Standing in front of this makeshift cubicle was a bosomy woman, her physique well-endowed enough to block the changing cubicle from peeping eyes. There, Lizzie met Alba the costume lady, broad smile on her face, with some of her front teeth missing. Alba turned out to be the sweetest of ladies, a nurturing mother to the cast. She grabbed Lizzie and pulled her close to her big buxom. Pinching Lizzie's cheeks, a stream of Spanish flowed from her mouth:

"La chica, flaca, guapa, la chica."

Lizzie had no idea what she was saying, but she thought in her twenty years, she had never felt such affection even from her own mother. With that began Lizzie's experience of costume fitting. Lizzie could sense Alba's exasperation as she continued to cluck like a mother hen:

"Dios mio! chichita."

Alba was having difficulty fitting the top of the diamante bikini on Lizzie because of her small bust, flat like a pancake. After more tutting and lots of alterations to the outfit, Alba finally got the bikini top to fit Lizzie. The bikini fitting was the most humiliating thing Lizzie had gone through; she just wanted the floor to open up and swallow her.

Next, a gigantic headdress with a huge nest of feathers on top of it was shoved on her head. Lizzie almost toppled over with the weight. She looked at the reflection in the mirror and saw the sparkling diamantes that had been individually sewn on to the headdress. The green feathers were meticulously sewn together, not one single feather out of place. A feathered collar went round the shoulders and was fixed on to her bikini bra strap. The softness of the feathers felt like silk to her touch. Finally, a three-piece feathered tail was attached to the base of her bikini bottom.

Although Lizzie was blown away by the luxurious and exquisite detail of the costumes, she could not help thinking:

"I have come all the way to Mexico to appear in a Vegas-like show."

She was then presented with a pair of six-inch heels.

"How the heck am I expected to dance in those heels on a cheap metal flooring?" she thought with dismay!

After the initial slow start, the costume fitting accelerated. Alba appeared to have by then computerized Lizzie's measurements in her brain. Soon Lizzie was decked with six different costumes of different styles from different decades, all made to a remarkably high standard, with exquisite fur and flashy diamantes of difference sizes. There was a feel of no expense-spared glamour to the whole thing. Lizzie soon forgot the discomfort of the fitting session and became completely mesmerized by the incredible costumes. If it was not for the fact that she was standing in a tent, Lizzie could easily have believed that she was going to appear in a high-budget Broadway or West-end show.

Finally, when the costume fitting was over, Alba gathered Lizzie in her huge bosom, and giving her a squeeze and a kiss, clucked:

"Manana! Gracias Chiquita." "Tomorrow! Thank you little one."

These were the first Spanish words Lizzie learned.

After a long, tedious wait whilst all the new girls had all their costumes fitted, with no offer of a drop of water, the girls were ushered into the same minibus that brought them to the circus and taken back to the hotel. Lizzie sat with her new good friend Karen. Poor Karen's ears were still hurting. Lizzie wondered if Karen was thinking the same despondent thoughts that were flashing across her jet lagged mind:

"The audition in London was nothing like what happened today! What the sweet Jesus is happening?"

Although Lizzie was relieved to have arrived and met with the other dancers, she was also anticipating what was to come as the reality slowly hit that she was not going to be dancing in a show in a Mexican theatre, as originally thought when they left London.

CHAPTER 2

The Bubbles Burst

"De Nuevo! De Nuevo! Again!"

Roberto shouted repeatedly in Spanish. Lizzie could hear the shouting, could see Roberto's hands flapping around, but she had no idea what he was saying. Roberto paced up and down the stage, cigarette holder dangling from his mouth. Lizzie was exhausted from the long rehearsals. They had already rehearsed three numbers; the company had been at it for three hours without any break. It was dark, there was no air. Lizzie did not know if she should laugh or cry at the ridiculous routines they have been made to perform.

Maya, the wife of Gustavo, owner of the circus, was naturally the centre of attention, being the lead dancer in the number they were rehearsing. But she was also the weakest link. She was just not a particularly technical dancer. Jason, who hailed from Northern Ireland, and the weaker of the two male dancers in the cast, had been given the task to lift Maya in the Parisian Can-Can number. Jason's face showed utter despair as he attempted to lift her. Lizzie and the other dancers within ear shot heard him moaned:

"She is like a fecking sack of potatoes!"

"How am I going to do this three times?"

Lizzie and the rest of the girls tried to suppress their laughter at this very inelegant sight. Just when Lizzie thought the rehearsals were over, after Roberto had repeatedly put the cast through the Can-Can routine, she then realized that Roberto had left the opening number to last. As if slicing a cake, the company was separated onto each end of the wings. As Lizzie hesitated, one of the girls, Jenny, whispered to her:

"Follow my lead."

Lizzie, when she first met Jenny, discovered she was here on the same Equity contract. Jenny came with her best friend Sandra, who could have been her twin except that the latter had blond hair. Both were trained at the Royal Ballet School in London. Jenny, a dark brunette with elfin-like face has big, brown eyes, a small, up-turned nose and legs that seem to stretch forever. Lizzie was completely in awe of Jenny's technical ability as she followed behind her. She could not help wondering why this petite, Royal Ballet-trained dancer who could easily have become a principal soloist was here dancing in a circus. Or like Lizzie, was she here because she needed an Equity card to be able to work in the UK?

"One and two and three and four and…"

As Roberto counted the timing in his loud booming voice, the two groups of dancers came together in a semicircle and looped around the stage to form one long line, ending up at the front of the stage, with the instruction that they were to place one foot at the edge of the stage. As the girls walked on, the music began. Vegas Showgirl music blasted out of the speakers. Just as the girls were all lined up, the curtains were pulled open by two Mexican stagehands. Lizzie tried not to laugh at the sight of these two men clumsily and frantically pulling at the curtains as they tried at the same time to turn their heads to gawk at the dancers. To them, it must have been an amazing sight to see twenty-one girls, with the purest of pearly white skins, in skimpy diamanté-studded bikinis, towering feathered headdress, on six-inch heels, like flamingos standing still on one leg to conserve their body heat. Lizzie was nervous as she stood at the end of the line where she could easily fall off the side of the stage. When she looked down, she could see that if she lost her balance, it was a long way down. The music that blasted from the sound system sounded tinny and shrill. The two Mexican men gawked at the girls, mouths drooling. Lizzie found this highly hilarious. Desperately trying to stifle her laugh, but failing, she almost missed a step in those killer six-inch heels. Roberto clapped his hands again and shouted in exasperation:

"Repetir! Repetir!"

That was Lizzie's first rehearsal experience. Rehearsals over, the girls were told to go back to rest and to come back to enjoy the show that night. Although Lizzie felt suspicious about all that had happened so far, she could not help but be intrigued. She found herself looking forward to watching the show that evening. They were told to enjoy it as they would be performing it by Saturday. Roberto told the girls in that same monotonous tone, like a pre-recorded message on a telephone answering machine:

"You have two times to get it right on Saturday, four times on Sunday and no mistakes by Monday, or you are gone!"

Lizzie snorted:

"Who is he kidding with his threats when he can't even say

them properly with his thick accent! Where is he going to find any replacements in this god-forsaken backyard by Monday?"

Whatever happened, the new girls were here to stay.

After the first, gruelling rehearsal, the cast was taken back to the hotel. Exhausted, Lizzie collapsed into her bed and fell asleep almost instantly. Before long, the phone in her room began to ring shrilly. She answered the phone and was told by a stern, barking voice at the other end of the line to meet in the reception in ten minutes as they were being taken back to the circus. She quickly got ready and went down with the rest of the girls. Her stomach growled loudly as she wondered when they would be given the time to have a proper hot meal. The same dusty old bus arrived, and the girls were ushered in quickly. The bus pulled out sharply from the front of the hotel building, the tyres of the wheels squealing, and soon they were on a poorly-paved road. Bouncing wildly throughout the journey back to the circus, Lizzie stared out of the dirty window of the bus. She had never seen such poverty, even though she came from a poor background herself. Makeshift wooden houses with metal roofing lined the road, brightly coloured large tarpaulins were pulled over some of the roofs, probably to prevent rainwater leaking into the houses. Groups of middle-aged men sat around on low stools in front of the houses, smoking and chatting. Children, with no shoes on, played on the street, stopping in their tracks to look at the dusty old bus full of European ladies. They looked happy enough but undernourished. Lizzie knew what it was like to go hungry, with no food for days.

On arrival, Lizzie could see hundreds of people queuing to enter the tent. No money was being exchanged, it seemed the tickets were being given out for free. There was an exciting buzz of anticipation – children running around, men and women chatting loudly and gaily to each other. The men mostly wore plain T-shirts and slacks made of rough cotton; the women had brightly coloured huipil tunic blouses and thick furry skirts. Though clean looking, they did not look like your typical theatre audience back home in England; some children did not even have shoes on their feet.

The girls were taken toward the back of the tent and through the side entrance. Lizzie spotted a few men; they were dressed quite differently from the men in the audience that she saw outside the tent. Looking dubious these men were wearing big cowboy hats, expensive-looking jeans, and cowboy boots. Strangely, some of them were wearing sunglasses even though the sky was getting darker in the dusk light.

"They look like they are in the protection profession, rather mafia-like." Lizzie thought to herself.

As she glanced over, she could feel their dark eyes on her, their gaze piercing her soul. It made her feel quite uncomfortable.

The girls were shown to their seats, away from the crowd. Within a moment, music came blasting out from the huge speakers, but from the side, a small orchestra attempted to keep in time with the pre-recorded sounds. They tried to stay in tune but failed miserably. Lizzie could see how hard the dancers were doing their best to keep in time to the music and to ignore the cacophony coming from the ad-hoc orchestra. The audience was oblivious to the jarring performance from the orchestra and was whipped up into a frenzy, their awe-stricken gasps audible. Lizzie herself could not believe how glamourous the whole show was, as the dance numbers flowed smoothly from one to another. A sense of awe came over Lizzie, she could not believe she will soon be performing in this elaborately extravagant show. The cast looked splendid in the highly polished dance numbers. As she watched the performance, Lizzie could not help feeling that there was a sadness in Jenny's big, brown eyes, even though she had a broad smile pasted on her face. Back at the hotel, despite the cast's moans that there was still a whole week to go, and Jenny telling them that they would soon change their mind after dancing sixteen shows in a week, with one's feet covered in blisters, Lizzie and Karen's excitement at performing in the show could not be dampened.

At the end of the second day of rehearsal, Lizzie was exhausted and was more than ready to go back to the hotel to enjoy a hot bath. Jenny's words of caution the night before came back to Lizzie. However, Roberto had other ideas. He clapped his hands and pointed his long, yellow stained fingers at Lizzie, summoning her over to him. Lizzie acted surprised, then reluctantly went up to him. Roberto told her in a jittery voice that he wanted her to be in his Magic act. He seemed to have taken a shine to Lizzie, dismissing one of the older girls who normally starred in his Magic act. Lizzie was dismayed, realizing that she was not going to have a break. She was then told to go to Alba for costume fitting and to return for a late rehearsal.

Lizzie went to Alba, who stood there beaming at her, prattling in Spanish. Alba handed her the skimpiest diamante bikini and a headdress which had enormous bright red feathers. By that time, Alba had already magically memorized Lizzie's measurements and so the fitting did not take too long. Lizzie returned to the rehearsal, thankful that she did not have to wear the costume. Waiting for her on the stage were three other girls from the company, who, like Lizzie, were a mere size 8. On the stage was a huge box on a wheel. While Roberto sat having another cigarette, Lucy, one of the girls, explained to Lizzie how she should basically get into the second compartment inside the box, where she has to be scrunched up, like a foetus in a mother's womb. Jenny appeared on the stage, Roberto, gin and tonic in his other hand, gave some gibberish instruction; Jenny was to improvise some dance steps. She stepped onto the top of the box, folded herself into the box sideway. Lizzie was instructed at that point to get into the back of the four boxes all secretly partitioned. Jenny got into the compartment next to Lizzie, Lucy and Sandra went into the other two compartments. Lizzie did not know whether to laugh or cry at the absurdity of the scene. She got into her compartment and folded herself like a rag doll. Roberto got up and instructed two Mexican men to spin the box. As the girls lifted the partitions up, the curtains went back up, and four girls were magically revealed. What they forgot to tell Lizzie was that she would be put in the back of the box from the beginning of the act. Therefore, she would be screwed up like a piece of tissue paper for the whole duration. Depending on Roberto's spontaneous interactions with the audience, Lizzie could be in there for however long it took. Lizzie managed to do this act for a couple of weeks successfully. The day before, the cast had been told they would be leaving Mexico in two weeks' time to perform in several Central American countries. The Sunday shows were always the most difficult to get through due to the four performances.

The second to the last Sunday before leaving Mexico, the weather had been unbearably hot and humid. The night air was so still one could hardly breathe. Even the lions did not want to perform for Gustavo. The whole company was drained by the extreme heat. Lizzie could not bear the thought of being stuck in the box, especially if Roberto was going to be carried away by his own voice, endlessly droning on. She prayed that Roberto would cancel the act that evening. But of course, it did not happen. If we were in the U.K, Lizzie thought to herself, the extreme heat conditions would have been taken into consideration. But they were in Mexico!

Because Gustavo had had a hard time getting the lions to perform and the act ran over, Lizzie was taking her time to get changed into the costume for the Magic act. The voice of a stagehand screeched from the side of the trailer:

"Rapido! Rapido!"

Lizzie frantically got into her costume and ran to the back of the stage. Before she could wiggle herself properly into her rag doll position in the secret partition, the trolley was already being pushed onto the stage. Lizzie could not breathe, she started panicking. Sandra and Lucy kept telling Lizzie to calm down. Lizzie opened the side of the box a tiny bit to get some air. At that moment, one of the red feathers from her headdress popped out of the crack. Lizzie could hear the audience shouting gleefully:

"Farol! Bluff!"

The sweaty stagehands quickly pushed the trolley off the stage amidst the roar of laughter from the audience. Roberto was absolutely fuming. His magic illusion had never been ruined before. After that incident, he never spoke to Lizzie again, and she was replaced by another dancer for the Magic Act. She secretly concealed her relief at never having to perform in the darn act again.

During the last performance of that Sunday show, Donna was found throwing up at the back of the stage. She was one of two dancers in the Clown act, the main clown being Lilly. One of the stagehands, Rocco, shouted into the trailer that a girl was needed as the second clown. The costume and a big brightly coloured wig were then chucked into the trailer. Nobody wanted to do it, the girls ignored Rocco, pretending not to hear him. The clown costume remains in a desperate heap on the floor of the trailer. Dance captain Maya started telling Lizzie that she had to do it as she was the only one small enough to fit into Donna's costume. After the earlier disaster, Lizzie vehemently refused to do it. Maya screamed at her and she was made to put the costume on. Following Lilly reluctantly on to the stage, Lizzie was told to get into a cage and to pull a secret blind down. The music began. Lilly improvised some dance moves in front of the cage while Roberto addressed the audience in his flamboyant manner. Lilly stepped into the cage, and while still dancing and wiggling about in full view of the audience, she started to rant about an argument she had with her boyfriend. As Lilly got more worked up by her ranting, Lizzie hissed at her to stop moving so much as her wiggling was making it difficult for Lizzie to hold the blind down. Before Roberto had a chance to lower the curtain over the cage and spin it around to magically reveal two clowns, Lizzie lost her grip and the blind shot up revealing two clowns. Lizzie tried to hide behind Lilly, trying to mimic Lilly's movements, but the audience was already hooting with laughter. That second fiasco definitely put an end to Lizzie's career as a magician's assistant.

Ignoring Roberto's screams to see her, Lizzie ran back to the trailer when the curtains came down, as though she was being chased by a cackle of hyenas. As it was already quarter past ten in the evening and the show was running really late, Lizzie had to get ready for the final number of the evening. Fortunately for her, she had a little bit of time to get her breath back as Gustavo's lion act came before the dance finale.

After the final dance, the audience erupted with thunderous applause as the curtains closed. Lizzie, without taking off her make-up, rushed to get on the minibus, taking care to avoid any contact with Roberto. Huddled in her seat, Lizzie fought back tears of humiliation. She did not know how she had managed to get through the final number with Roberto's torrent of abuse ringing in her ears.

Arriving back at the hotel, Lizzie decided not to join the other girls for their regular after-the -show get together which usually took place in one of the girl's rooms. All she wanted to do is to crawl into bed and try to forget the fiasco of the evening's performances. Roberto's violent abuse brought back unpleasant memories of what she used to have to endure from her father. Just like in the past, she hoped that the stillness of the night would comfort her and help her to forget.

CHAPTER 3

The Bluff

The performances the following night went without a hitch, although there were lots of whispers that Lizzie had made a call to Equity, and someone said snidely that she would get into trouble. Even though Maya had screamed at her in between the numbers, accusing her of making the call, Lizzie remained tight-lipped. She couldn't understand how this had got out as she had been so careful when she sneaked downstairs in the middle of the night to make the call from the hotel reception. Alba had, now and again, warned her to be wary of the circus spies. She would say to Lizzie:

"Be careful, chica, be careful. There are spies everywhere!"

Maybe what Alba had been saying to her was true after all, Lizzie thought.

As Lizzie came down the steps of the trailer, still drained from the previous night's gruelling four shows and the debacles, one of Gustavo's men, who always had a gun on him, was standing there. He pointed at Lizzie:

"Not you, you come."

Lizzie rolled her eyes, thinking in her mind that Roberto

was still furious with her and that she must now go and face the music. She reluctantly followed him out of the circus tent, across the muddy field, to another trailer. She was told to sit down outside and wait. At first, it did not bother her. The longer she could delay the wrath of Roberto, the better it was. She watched as the stagehands did their usual clean-up, sweeping up the rubbish left by the audience. There was much raucous laughter and chattering from the men. They always seemed so carefree, Lizzie mused.

With all these distractions, Lizzie did not realize an hour had gone past. She began to feel cold. She was wearing only a thin top, shorts and sneakers. She was stiffening up, feeling rigor mortis setting in. Finally, the activities around her began to settle. Silence engulfed her as she sat there with her knees up to her chest and arms wrapped around herself. The door of the trailer flung open. She looked up, her eyes squinting from exhaustion. It was another one of those men, standing at the top of the stairs, wearing an open shirt with big lapels, tight jeans, he had big hands, great big sovereign rings on his fingers, big gold chain with a cross lying across his hairy chest. The man said something to her in Mexican. Lizzie did not understand. He then said:

"Come in.

Lizzie got up stiffly, climbing slowly up the stairs of the trailer, her mind still reeling with the disaster of the magic show and clown act. As she went up the stairs, the man did not move. She had to move sideways to get around him. She felt uneasy as she could smell his foul breath and the tension in his body as she brushed past him.

When she entered the trailer, it was like walking into a

luxurious hotel room – leather seats, drinks cabinet at the far end. Gustavo and four other men were in the trailer. Lizzie was a bit shocked:

"Where's Roberto? He is not in there."

Lizzie was told to sit down on one of the leather sofas. Lizzie sank right into the plush seat, her tiny frame was engulfed. It made her feel really small, rather like Goldilocks. She struggled to sit herself back up, trying to perch herself at the edge of the sofa and pulled herself up as much as she could. There was complete silence. It seemed to go on forever. All Lizzie could hear was the ticking of the clock on the wall, which seemed to her to be getting louder and louder. Those men just looked at her, sneeringly, chewing on their tobacco. Gustavo sat on one of the huge sofas, puffing away on his cigar. Lizzie gave them a haughty look, trying to give them the impression she was not afraid. Among them was the guy who recruited the dancers from London. He was the interpreter, suave-looking, smooth hands, clean fingers, a sign of someone who had never lifted a finger to do a day's work, very much the "Smooth Operator". He walked towards Lizzie, came to a halt in front of her and said:

"Gustavo wants to know why you called Equity."

Lizzie looked back at him, and with a tilt of her chin, said defiantly:

"Because I can."

The Smooth Operator related it back to Gustavo, who then said something to him in Spanish. Smooth Operator turned and said to Lizzie:

"You have caused a lot of trouble by doing this."

With much bravura, Lizzie retorted:

"I have not. I am here on an Equity contract, so I can call

them if I want to."

He repeated it to Gustavo in Spanish. Gustavo smashed his fist down on the table. Everyone jumped. He then pointed at Lizzie and said in a loud agitated voice:

"You do what we ask you to do, where we ask you to go."

Lizzie, still defiant, jumped up from the seat and said:

"No I'm not! I am contracted to Mexico only. You can't make me go elsewhere."

As Lizzie stood there, fists clenched, nobody in the room made a sound. The silence was deadly. The ticking sounds of the clock seemed to get louder in Lizzie's head. She looked around the room, her bravado was beginning to slip away. She could see from the side of her eyes the two men by the door looking nervous, sweat was breaking out around their foreheads. Gustavo exploded with anger, swearing in rapid Italian, like one of his lions roaring. Lizzie could see the scars from being mauled by the lions blazoned across his chest as his shirt was opened. All the other men did not know where to look, they appeared nervous. For a moment, Lizzie was afraid, frightening thoughts flashed through her mind – was she going to be bundled into a car and made to disappear? Would they feed her to the lions? But just as quickly, she stopped panicking. She thought this whole scene was quite funny. She had had no food all evening, her hair was all messed-up, she was so tired and exhausted that she was not quite herself. She was not fazed by Gustavo's angers. After all, she was quite used to this kind of explosive situations with her father. She had learned not to let it bother her. The Smooth Operator began to speak:

"Gustavo says you are going to be sent to a shit circus in Mexico and no one will know where you've gone. Gustavo will not be responsible for you there. Anything can happen to you."

Lizzie looked at the Smooth Operator and said:

"No he won't! You tell Gustavo that like him, I have a family in London, and my family won't like that. Do you know who my family is related to? Do you know who the Kray twins are? Tell Gustavo that."

Lizzie reeled off a few other crime families in London. "My godfather is Bernie Silver. You send me to Shit Circus, they will come for you. I don't think that they are going to like that."

The mention of the Kray twins seemed to have worked the trick. There was a frantic discussion between Gustavo, the Smooth Operator and a few of the men. Gustavo then summoned Lizzie to him. Lizzie walked up to him, her make up running, hair in a loose, untidy bun, and stood arms crossed, in front of Gustavo. Gustavo stared at her. His hands were so big he could have killed her easily, Lizzie thought. He sat back on the chair, his big stomach lolling, looked her up and down, as if he were sizing her up or chewing on what she had said. After what seemed like eternity, Gustavo spoke, in English:

"Equity says you can go to Central America."

He repeated it. Lizzie said:

"I want to speak to Equity to confirm this."

Gustavo's eyes narrowed, and he said:

"Tomorrow, you can speak to Equity. Now, no more trouble. Go!"

Lizzie couldn't believe Gustavo fell for her bluff. She gleefully thought to herself:

"I should have been an actress rather than a dancer."

But then when the men were driving her back to the hotel, she wondered why Gustavo changed his mind. Maybe it was only a temporary arrangement that she would remain with the circus; they might still come back for her at a later date. Fear engulfed her, but sheer exhaustion took over and she was just relieved, for now, that she'd got away with it.

The next morning, Lizzie was hauled out of bed early. The smooth Operator was waiting for her at the hotel reception. He took her to an office with a telephone. On the telephone, waiting to speak to Lizzie, was someone from Equity. A silky-smooth voice with an English accent on the phone said to Lizzie:

"It is safe for you to go to Central America. You would be well looked-after."

On hearing from Equity that it would be alright, Lizzie felt more reassured.

The days flew by, and soon it was the last Sunday before the circus was due to leave Mexico for Guatemala, their first stop in Central America. Lizzie dreaded the fact that they must pack their bags and come back to the circus with their suitcases after the gruelling four shows. Although nobody said anything, there was an air of slight uncertainty among the cast as it is their last performance in Mexico. They have still not received a new contract from Equity giving written permission to travel into Central America.

As they got close to the final acts of the very final show in Mexico, Lizzie was changing into her costume for the closing dance number, which followed Gustavo's lion act. Lizzie could hear the lions growling in anticipation. It sounded somewhat different this time, Lizzie thought, as she pulled on her slinky silver diamante bikini that was designed to ensure they don't put on any weight. She then pulled up her double fishnet tights because her bikini bottom was so revealing. She looked in the mirror and retouched her make up. She gathered her pink feather robe around her shoulders and started her way down the steps of the trailers to join the other girls in the wings for the last number. As she approached, the roars of the lions were deafening. She could hear Maya screaming:

"Stop Gustavo! Alto!"

Lizzie got to the wings and craned her neck to see what was going on. To her absolute astonishment, Gustavo was in the cage with all the lionesses; they were conceding to his every command like docile domestic cats. At the same time, all the stagehands were crowding in front of the cage, frantically shouting. They looked terrified. Gustavo cracked his whip loudly. Lizzie looked at the direction of his whip and saw this huge mane, and sat on the top tier was the most majestic lion that Lizzie had ever seen. She wondered out loud:

"Where did this lion come from?"

Lizzie had never seen this lion in any of the performances. Tammy whispered:

"This is the lion that nearly mauled Gustavo to death. But Gustavo never had him put down and has kept the lion on almost like a pet."

The majestic beast stared down at Gustavo from his great height. Lizzie could see its eyes narrowing, as though it was eyeing Gustavo like he was its next meal. Lizzie had heard through the grapevine that Gustavo was not happy that they were leaving Mexico. He did not want his circus to go to Central America. Lizzie wondered if all this act of bravura and putting himself at risk came out of the frustrations he was feeling about being told they have to go to Central America. Was he trying to prove he was in control?

Gustavo's screaming jolted Lizzie out of her thoughts. He was screaming for the stagehands to bring the meat in. The four stagehands were shoving each other, none of whom clearly wanted to be the one to go into the cage with the meat. After some tussle among the four guys, the shortest and the stoutest guy was pushed forward, his fat belly flopping into the cage first. He stealthily stepped toward Gustavo with the pole on which the meat was strung at the end. Gustavo grabbed the pole impatiently from him and pushed it upward toward the roaring lion. All the other lionesses were cowered down, seemingly confused. The lion went up on its hind legs, jumped off the stool toward Gustavo. Gustavo teased him with the meat as it moved closer toward him. The audience was up on their feet, the atmosphere changed from a raucous one to complete silence; some had their jaws wide open, staring unbelievably at what was happening. Gustavo dropped down to his knees with the pole with the meat beside him, the lion came up to him and as Gustavo lowered his head, the lion approached him, putting its head right up to Gustavo's face – in a split second their faces almost touched. The audience gasped! The lion went for the meat. Gustavo jumped up, his arms wide open. He looked triumphant as though to prove that he was in charge.

Before Lizzie could question what she had just seen, the music for the final number began. All the girls stepped onto the stage in their resplendent costumes and high heels. The atmosphere was electrifying and the audience were almost in a frenzy after witnessing Gustavo's daredevil act. The dancers too, were swept up in that moment, giving it their all. The audience had always loved the finale, but that night, it was even more so. It looked like this last show given in this small border town in Mexico would go down in history. The circus and this final show would be spoken about by the villagers for many years to come.

CHAPTER 4

The Circus Rolls on

Late that evening, Lizzie and the rest of the cast left Mexico for Central America. After hanging around for about two hours in the freezing cold, waiting for the tents to be taken down, everyone's attention was drawn to watching the dismantling of the huge tent which collapsed like a pack of cards. It was quite incredible to watch, as the little Mexican men had no sophisticated tools, they were just doing it manually with huge thick ropes. Another group of men were shouting to these stagehands with such aggression that Lizzie could see the frightened look on their faces. Lizzie's eyes moved over to a huge truck. She saw several men on their knees. They had blowtorches in their hands, and were opening the metal part of the wheels of the truck. It was too far for Lizzie to see clearly what exactly they were doing, but she could make out that they were putting some things into the rims of the wheels. Lizzie wondered why there was so much shouting and frantic urgency to it all.

Finally, they were allowed on the coach. Without much conversation, the cast members settled into their seats and the lights went out. The coach travelled through the night towards the border of Mexico and Guatemala. Just at sunrise, the coach arrived at the Mexican border of Tabasco near the Usumacinta River.

At the border, just before the crossing, the cast requested a toilet break. The toilet was manned by a toothless Mexican. It was utterly revolting, more a hole in the floor, smeared with faeces, than a toilet. One of the girls went in and ran out disgusted. No way was Lizzie going to go in there. She walked up the side of the river, found a bush and started to do her business. As she stooped in the bush, she looked up and saw men with guns pointing at her, helicopters were hovering overhead, whirring above her. She panicked and finished up quickly, pulling her knickers up and running back to the coach as quickly as she could.

The coach crossed the border into Guatemala. The journey thereafter went quickly on the smooth, tarmac road. Soon they were travelling in a built-up area. Some of the houses seemed well-built, unlike in Mexico. Lizzie was somewhat disconcerted to see droves of armed soldiers on the streets. They were surrounded by plainly-dressed women and children wearing no shoes, who were selling food and drinks or folk trinkets. Whenever the coach stopped at a traffic light, these women and children would rush up to the windows and try to sell their wares. Lizzie smiled to herself, thinking ironically that she was probably just as poor as them. But in their eyes, they were probably white American tourists whom they think have lots of money.

Arriving at the hotel, which looked rundown and drab, they were told by Maya the dance captain that they would have to share rooms. Lizzie and Karen paired up and when they got to their room, they were dismayed at the sight of the shabby room – single beds with rather filthy-looking sheets, a wash basin, there was no heating and the running water was lukewarm. Lizzie tried to cheer Karen up, fishing out a small bottle of disinfectant from her case. Together they stripped their beds and gave them a good, vigorous wiping down. When it was all done, Lizzie beamed:

"No fleas will survive this!"

Feeling hungry, they then went down to see if there was a place to buy hot food. One of Gustavo's men sitting by the door got up and walked toward them, saying in broken English:

"No allow, no go out."

He pointed to a room where they could go and get sandwiches which had been laid out for the cast. Lizzie and Karen went in and was none too happy that there were only cold sandwiches and bottled water. In the room was a sign saying they had to be ready by three o'clock for the coach that was taking them to the circus.

During the journey to the circus, Maya announced that there would be hot food served after the show that evening. They were also warned that they were not allowed to wander on their own into the city after the show. Shortly the coach pulled into a rather isolated field where Lizzie could see the finishing touches being done to the tent. Lizzie was not really fazed by the increased security and number of guards surrounding the tent as she had already seen the huge number of soldiers on the streets earlier.

After the first performance that evening, there was a barbeque and a few men were standing before the pits cooking the food. There was music and the food and drinks flowed.

For the first time, the cast mixed with the stagehands, eating their barbequed food, drinking, talking and even dancing to the music. At one point, Lizzie's eyes almost popped out when she turned around and saw Kimberly and Tracey picking up the rifles that the guards have left lying on the floor, posing and laughing, totally oblivious to the reality of the dangers that they might be in. In the first few shows, the audience number was small, but by the end of the week, the shows were packed out again as more people came. This prevailed in the second week of the performances.

Whilst the barbeque and the food after the show in the first few days were fantastic, the novelty wore off as it went on, the choice on offer becoming less and less. It became wearying for the cast. It was no longer as fun standing around in the cold waiting for the food to be cooked. By this time, several of the girls had been badly bitten by bed bugs. A few of them suffered terribly from the bites, with arms, legs and even the face, covered with red and angry lumps. It was so bad that Roberto was forced to cut the number of dancers in the opening and closing numbers as the skimpy costumes exposed the unsightly pustules on the dancers' body, ruining the illusion of the pure, white, unblemished, porcelain-like skin. Fortunately, Lizzie and Karen were saved by her disinfectant and also thanks to Alba the costume lady, Lizzie was able to get another bottle to keep the bugs away.

Finally, the two-week performance schedule in Guatemala came to an end. There was an excitement in the air; word has got out that Gustavo was so pleased with the shows that he made a point to get on the coach before leaving for Honduras, their next scheduled stop. He sheepishly apologised for the state of the hotel, trying to explain that there was a mix-up with the hotel booking. He then reassured the company that they would be staying in a nice hotel in Honduras. Rumours had gone round that the hotel was going to be magnificent.

The coach spluttered into action and off they went on the next leg of their journey. Whenever they travelled, Lizzie always insisted she took a small case with her (with her supply of tampons). Being a Catholic country, it was difficult to get tampons anywhere, so it was a bit of a trade off with the rest of the girls.

As the coach continued on its way, the terrain started to change from an urban surrounding to dirt track roads. All of a sudden, the driver braked hard and the coach came to a violent halt, causing everyone to lurch forward and immediately fall back to their seats. Lizzie looked out of the window. There was thick fauna all around, much like a jungle. It looked menacing and dark. Lizzie thought:

"There is literally nowhere to run if something happened."

All of a sudden, the door was yanked opened. Lizzie peered out of the window to see that the coach was surrounded by men in khaki green, almost like a soldier's uniform. They all carried guns and weapons. There was a lot of shouting and some held their guns up in the air, firing shots randomly. A soldier with a machine gun came on the bus. He stood in the front of the bus, big and burly, dark, olive brown skin, with a green beret sitting on his head. He appeared to be in charge, just like a general. Lizzie looked at him, he had a prevalent scar down the side of his cheek. His wide, square jaw was almost hidden by his unruly beard, like the dense jungle surrounding them. When he spoke, one could see a flash of a gold tooth. He shouted at the driver and slapped him on the head with his gun. He bellowed down the bus: "No speak! Shut up." He then walked down the narrow aisle of the coach. Lizzie could feel the heat of his breath on her head. She was overwhelmed by the feeling of helplessness and she simply froze. One of the dancers, Chloe, started to whimper. He shouted at her to shut up. Petrified, Chloe cried, her sobs getting louder. He grabbed her by her long, golden ponytail, and yanked her off her seat, pinning her down on the floor of the bus. One of the soldiers rushed up the bus and started to drag Chloe off the bus. Chloe started to scream hysterically, all the dancers in the bus, too, started to scream at the men to let Chloe go. The youngest dancer of the group Kimberly stood in her seat and shouted: "Leave her alone!" as she rained her fists on the soldier's back, trying to stop him from dragging Chloe off the bus. Kimberly's fists on his back did nothing, the soldier did not even once flinch. In desperation, Kimberly shouted:

"You don't know who we are, you don't know who our boss is! He is going to kill you!"

Another solider boarded the bus, pointing his machine gun at the girls. Lizzie was completely frozen with fear, wondering what the hell was happening. All she could do was move her gaze to the window and saw Chloe being pushed to the ground. The soldiers surrounded her, using their guns to try and lift her skirt up. She looked like a trapped animal, ready to be slaughtered. Lizzie found herself wondering:

"Real soldiers don't behave like this, surely? Maybe these are the bandits spoken about in the rumours."

Other soldiers came on the bus, they shouted to the girls: "Stay there, don't move!"

They grabbed the cases and started tipping things out. They

grabbed Lizzie's case and found all the neatly packed tampons in the case. They took them all out and started tearing them up and sniffing at them. Lizzie looked at them in dismay:

"That's my cash flow going up in smoke!"

The tampons were strewn everywhere. Lizzie could hear all the dancers starting to scream and cry hysterically. The boss soldier appeared to be losing control, he shouted again, trying to get them to quieten down. Another soldier came up and spoke frantically in Spanish to him. Before he could finish, as if in Roberto's magic act, a guy in civilian garb then got on the bus. He called to the leader of the group, spoke in a firm and controlled manner to him in Spanish, and in a flash, the soldiers disappeared as quickly as they had appeared. Lizzie bent down to pick up all the tampons. To her relief, they only destroyed half of them, and there were still some left intact. Chloe was shoved roughly back up onto the coach. The head girl Olivia went to her and gently calmed her, trying to reassure her that everything was now okay. She sat next to Chloe for the rest of journey, tenderly soothing her, trying to calm her hysterical sobbing. As the coach drove off, she could see the soldiers staring at them. One of them spat on the floor.

For the remainder of the journey, Karen and Lizzie cuddled up to each other in silence, as do the rest of the cast. The coach proceeded towards the border to cross into Honduras, with its passengers in the state of bewilderment and disbelief, some still shaking visibly from the unexpected turn of events. Suddenly, their excitement at leaving Guatemala to enter Central America dissipated. The naivety of the situation that they found themselves in began to sink in. They had thought that everything would be fine as they believed Equity UK told them that it was okay for them to go there. Lizzie thought back to the telephone call with Equity that was arranged while they were still in Mexico, it suddenly dawned on her it was just a voice on the phone. There was nothing written in black and white that the whole cast was safe to leave Mexico to travel with the circus to Central America. She could not believe how stupid she has been.

After experiencing an awfully long wait at the Guatemala-Honduras border, they were finally allowed to cross. Gustavo kept his promise, the hotels they were put in were absolutely beautiful, but the shell-shocked cast remained sombre. They arrived with American helicopters whirring in the air, circling the hotel. Before Lizzie went to her room, she decided to ask at the reception why there were helicopters circling the hotel. The receptionist explained in halting English that US troops were ordered into Honduras to support the government to prevent more Nicaraguan soldiers from crossing the border. The girls had no idea of the political situation. There were oblivious to the dangers they might be in. By now, they had all somewhat calmed down after the incident at the border. They were just so excited at seeing the beautiful hotel, after the dire place they had been in. Lizzie was particularly excited as her twenty-first birthday was approaching.

There was no show that evening and there was no rehearsal the next day as they had a travel day. Lizzie had a luxurious lie in that morning in her beautiful hotel room, with the huge double bed all to herself, a nice bathroom – she even had a personal maid who kept coming in to bring her fresh towels. After her shower, the bed was already beautifully made. She had never experienced such service before, she felt like royalty. The maid probably earned the same amount as what she was earning as a dancer, but the maid was full of deference. She lapped it all up, determined to make the most of it. Lizzie pointed to the television and asked the maid in her broken Spanish about the men in official suits also carrying firearms seen in the hotel lobby and the guerrilla fighters on the TV. The maid gestured and spoke rapidly, Lizzie could only understand the words:

"American hombre, Guatemala army, not want American soldiers."

Lizzie could just about make out that a coup was happening in some parts of Central America and that the Honduras government had requested help from the United States and that the U.S. President ordered more than 3000 troops into Honduras. The news was reporting that Nicaraguan soldiers had crossed its borders.

The phone in the room started to ring. A voice spoke and said:

"Roberto has requested a cast meeting. You are to get ready and go in for a last-minute rehearsal."

Before leaving for the rehearsal, Lizzie spoke to the hotel maid and bribed her to buy some party food and alcohol for a birthday party she was going to spring on the cast. Lizzie was so happy she didn't mind that she had to go in for a rehearsal even though it was her birthday.

After the rehearsal, they returned to the hotel. As planned earlier with Karen, the girls went to the spa and swimming pool in the basement. It was enclosed in glass, as they swam, they could see helicopters still flying above the hotel. Disconcerting as it might be, it didn't spoil their enjoyment of giving themselves a treat.

Returning to her room after the swim, Lizzie took a nap. Later on, they were going to meet with the other girls in the bar although they had been told they were not allowed to go to the hotel bar. For a change, Lizzie was going to throw caution to the wind and break the rules. After all, it was her twenty-first birthday, she was allowed to be naughty for a change.

After the nap, Lizzie started putting on her dress and make-up. Staring at herself in the mirror, she was amazed at how beautiful she is. She had never thought of herself as that. Many women would have killed to have her looks.

There was a knock on her door. She opened the door and all the girls shouted "Surprise!" They piled into her large room, more like a mini apartment really. Somebody put the music on, and several of the girls brought bottles of beer, coca cola, whilst others brought nibbles. Lizzie got birthday cards from the girls. She was quite overwhelmed. She had never ever had a birthday party in her life. Everyone started dancing, chatting, laughing. Although they did not have much in terms of food and drinks, it was the best time Lizzie had ever experienced.

There was another knock on the door. The American girl Tammy shouted: "I'll get this." When she opened the door, two of Gustavo's men from the circus stood at the door. Lizzie thought with dismay, they had come to stop the party. To her surprise, they brought a box full of drinks – beers, soft drinks – and what's more, a huge birthday cake with loads of fruits piled on top of colourful icing and decorations. Lizzie was so taken aback. One of the girls said mockingly:

"Gustavo's moved on."

Something made Lizzie look over at Kimberly. Kimberly stared back at Lizzie with her piercing eyes. Lizzie said:

"No, he was probably just making amends for keeping me back in the trailer."

Lizzie thought to herself: "no way was I going to sleep with that big fat beast."

The girls all dived into the cake and within minutes it was all devoured. There was a knock on the door again. This time, it was the maid, a big smile on her face, who came bearing the food and drinks that Lizzie has asked for earlier. This went down as an extra treat and was enjoyed by all. Eventually the party ended as quickly as it started as they knew tomorrow brought another day – early start with the rehearsal, and the opening night of fourteen long hard shows ahead.

The opening performances went without a hitch. By this time, the cast had nailed the dance numbers, and the audience loved the razzle dazzle. There were rumours that Kimberly was having an affair with Gustavo. The girls had a great time gossiping about it. Lizzie was not shocked by this news. There was a friction between Kimberly and Gustavo's wife Maya. Just before the last show on the Sunday, Kimberly decided she was not going to perform the Russian number. She had a huge row with the head girl Olivia, so she came up with the excuse that she had a stomach ache. A quick change of staging was needed to cover her. That was the beginning of Kimberly's tantrums and demands as she believed that her status had changed due to her affair with the owner of the circus, which entitled her to do exactly as she pleased. Lizzie found this amusing, a genuinely nice distraction from the monotony of performing the same dance routine, day in, day out, for the past five and a half months – like Groundhog Day. Kimberly's tantrums, the friction between Maya and Kimberly, added a little sparkle to

Lizzie's humdrum life. Despite all the tensions and dramas, Honduras was the best tour stop they had – the performances were great, the hotel was the nicest of all, and to top it all, Lizzie celebrated her special birthday.

Sunday night rolled by again. Reluctantly they went back to the hotel, packed up their suitcases, and took them back to the circus grounds. They went back to their nice hotel for the last night. Lizzie took the advantage of enjoying the fabulous hotel facilities. She took a long bath, languishing in the luxuriousness of it. She had a feeling in her stomach, a foreboding. She sensed a different atmosphere in the circus. Somethings felt heavy in the air (perhaps due to the constant drones of the helicopters).

Lizzie's gut feelings came true. The San Salvador hotel was a drop in standard from the hotel in Honduras. It was more like a low-grade motel – the rooms were dark, basic, unwelcoming. It was a bit of a come down after Honduras. The dancers' spirits lifted when they discovered a Dunkin Donut shop two doors down from the hotel. The dingy motel did not matter anymore. They were informed that they would be picked up the next morning for rehearsals, as the new girls had arrived.

Lizzie now felt she was an old hand. She had to help rehearse the new girls into the dance routines. Lizzie and Karen got up early and enjoyed a Dunkin Donut each, almost missing the coach that would take them to the circus. They arrived for rehearsals, waiting on stage. Roberto came on stage and spoke; 'These are the new girls', waving vaguely to the back of the audience seats. The girls squinted to look at the new girls in the dim lights. Lizzie thought:

"Some of them do not look like dancers."

Then all of a sudden, Lizzie saw at the back of the

auditorium, somebody she knew – Mandy, with whom she trained at her old dancing school. Sitting next to Mandy was Lucy, with whom Lizzie went to Miss Jean's dancing school when she was younger. Lizzie could not believe her eyes. She was so excited to see them. Before the rehearsals started, the girls told her that they had been brought from the other circus show in Mexico City. They were introduced to the other new girls. The rehearsal with the new girls was really draining. Roberto worked the new girls really hard. Lizzie felt sorry for Mandy, as she was an awkward dancer, not comfortable with her own body. Amongst the new girls was one from Belgium. She did not have a dancer's legs, was a little heavyset, with a pear-shaped body. The circus was having a grand opening on Saturday night. But for some reason, of which the company was not told, the Saturday performance was cancelled. This meant the cast had a bonus day off.

Lizzie, Karen, Susan, Jason, Brian and Ellie decided they were going to explore San Salvador. They got up early in the morning, left the hotel, not before they had their nice coffee and donuts from Dunkin Donuts. They went to the bus station, managed to get tickets to go to the Seaside. They sat on a bus, with local people staring at them as though they were from outer space. The girls wore shorts, tight tee shirts, and Jason was in his tight hot pants. As the bus left the city, Lizzie saw the poverty around her, many lived in small huts, children with dirty hair, no shoes, little girls, holding babies. It came as a shock to Lizzie, although money was tight growing up and she often went to bed with a rumbling belly, she had never had to go without shoes. The bus went off on a dirt road full of potholes. At one point, Lizzie looked out of the window of the bus, she saw in between some palm trees a huge house, like a plantation house. It was really rundown. In front of the house stood a little emaciated black girl with no shoes on her feet. Behind her sat a Latin-American woman with a baby on her lap. She looked across at the bus and Lizzie met her blank gaze. Lizzie heard the sounds of the waves through the half-open window in the bus. She sat up excitedly.

Soon, the bus dropped them off at this beautiful beach with the whitest of sand and clear blue sea. Everyone made a dash for the sea. After a short swim, Jason wandered off to explore. He came back beaming with confidence and told them to follow him. He had found a shack and there was an elderly man who was pleased to see them. He brought out some bottles of Coca-Cola, they sat on a log, happily sipping the coke even though there was no ice. The old man said he could cook them some fish. They negotiated a price for the meal. When he brought the plate of fried fish, Lizzie couldn't eat them – they were so small and full of bones. She had thought they were going to get something like fish and chips at home. The guys, however, happily tucked into them.

Before they know it, the sun was setting. They found themselves having to run for the last bus leaving the beach to make it back to the city, not realizing that the next day, they were going to be subjected to a torrent of abuse for simply escaping for a day.

After a long day out, they made their way back to the hotel. They got picked up the next day for an early rehearsal. When they got off the coach, they were told to go into the circus tent and wait. After about ten minutes, 'Smooth Operator' made an appearance. He began screaming and shouting at them:

"You idiots! You could have been kidnapped; it is not a safe place to wander off on your own. Anything could have happened!"

Lizzie had never experienced such rage. He told them in no uncertain terms that they should never go off on their own again, they must always stay in the circus so that they would be protected. Lizzie could not understand why he made such a big deal about it and why he was going on about protection. She wondered what they were being protected from. The girls looked at each other with raised eyebrows, not understanding why they were subjected to such a tirade. Unbeknown to them, they were so naïve and oblivious to the dangers that they could have faced.

That evening's performance sailed through as if someone had their finger on a fast forward button. The cast was instructed after the show to go back to the hotel, pack their things immediately and to come straight back to the circus.

"Vamos! Vamos!"

Smooth operator shouted.

Lizzie had by now picked up a little more Spanish, and the word that she was constantly hearing was 'vamos' 'let's go'. There was definitely a change in the atmosphere and some urgency was felt.

Lizzie learnt that the circus trailers were going through Nicaragua, but the cast was going to fly from San Salvador to Costa Rica.

Arriving in Costa Rica, the journey from the airport to the city was quite exciting. It was such a change from the poverty-stricken cities of San Salvador. They were now travelling through a vibrant, wealthy, and an Americanised city: there were huge advertising bill boards everywhere, and even a McDonalds. Entering the city, Lizzie saw fancy skyscrapers and lush hotels. Arriving at what she thought was the hotel at which they were going to stay, waiting for them in the hotel reception was the Smooth Operator. The cast was given their pay of 80,000 pesos. He told them they would have to find their own accommodation and also make their own way to the circus for the performances each night. With that, the Smooth Operator fluffed off and left the group standing there rather bewildered by this sudden change of control and their newfound freedom!

At this point, the new Belgian dancer Juliette spoke up and said:

"Don't worry, I've arranged for an apartment for us all."

In the group were Brian, Jason, Matias, Lizzie, Karen, Ellie, Susan, Elen, Amelia, Chloe, Lucy and Olivia. They got into several taxis and off they went to the new apartments, which was across town. Lizzie and Karen quickly settled into their new apartment and went off to enjoy a lovely afternoon, planning to go to the zoo and the food market. They laughed at how so many of the restaurants look like 1950s American diners. Feeling hungry, Lizzie and Karen decided to go for a hamburger and soda. Enjoying the music from the jukebox, they threw caution to the wind, not caring a tot about their diet as in the past 7 months they had been put on a strict diet, not being allowed to put on weight to ensure they could get into their costumes as there was no room for alterations or change of costumes. Lizzie often lost a lot of weight, due to the brutality of the performance schedule. They had such a great time they did not want the day to end. Before making their way back to the apartment, they decided to go to the local flea market to buy presents to take back to England. They giggled to themselves as men who walked past them called out:

"American dollar! Por favor, dollar!"

Lizzie laughed and replied:

"Non, segnor, Inglias chica! Descuento muchas gracias!", whilst Karen called out cheekily trying to see if they can get a good bargain: "El dinero en menos, por favor!"

Back at their apartment, still elated from their carefree day, they found a note on the kitchen table, telling them to go to the first apartment next door. Lizzie and Karen looked at each other quizzically. Entering the apartment, they saw everyone huddled around. Juliette, the Belgian girl was holding court. She was talking animatedly about Gustavo and the circus; that they are in danger, and the authorities are on to them. She spoke with certainty that very soon they would all be sent home. The rest of the cast had no idea what she was on about.

Later that evening, Juliette requested that we join her in her apartment for a social gathering. Jason squealed delightfully:

"Oh! A party! Fabulous. Better to trash her apartment than mine."

Lizzie and Karen looked forward to it, but they decided that they were not going to drink too much as Lizzie could not hold her drink and there was going to be a rehearsal in the morning. They did not want to upset Roberto the next day.

When they entered Juliette's apartment, there was no party atmosphere. Instead, the rest of the cast was sitting there looking rather solemn. Juliette was holding court and telling everybody that she is here not just as a dancer but working for a European agency, without adding any details. She was kind of talking in riddles. She kept saying that the people she worked for will protect them from Gustavo and the circus. In Lizzie's mind, they have always been protected by the circus. She was baffled. Juliette continued to talk about drugs, going on about Drug Cartels and firearms. She kept referring to the CIA. Lizzie and Karen exchanged looks, whispering 'CIA? What is she on about?'

Lizzie looked around at the rest of the group. Nobody seemed to know what Juliette was referring to. Juliette repeated that this was an ongoing operation, working with people from different countries. Jason finally stood up and said:

"I have had enough of all this crazy talk. Let us have a party."

Juliette looked put out that what she had said did not seem to be taken very seriously by the cast and nobody was concerned and seemed not to believe her. The cast thought:

"We are just dancers here on an equity contract. What do we know about drug cartels and the struggle of the freedom fighters in Central America?"

That night was spent talking and listening to the stories of the new people, getting to know them, having fun, drinking, dancing, and mimicking Roberto and his ungainly gait.

The next day, Lizzie was woken up by loud banging on the door. She opened the door and squinted at the bright sunlight, a little hung over. Standing there was one of Gustavo's security men. He said abruptly to Lizzie that they must be ready for rehearsals at 10am. They had to find their own way there. The cast arranged for taxis on their own. To Lizzie's surprise the ride to the circus went very smoothly.

When they arrived at the circus, there was a different atmosphere. The older girls, Tammy, Amelia, Stacey, except Kimberly, were already there, looking miserable. Simone rushed over to Kimberly to tell her the news about the new apartment. Roberto stormed in, no niceties. It was like he had a bullet in his backside. He shouted at the company aggressively. He was nasty to the new girls, very dismissive of them. By now, Lizzie and the older girls know the routines like the back of their hands. For the new girls, it seemed exceedingly difficult. Lizzie could see that Juliette was not a very natural dancer. She looked distracted, more interested in her surroundings than in the dancing. She wanted to sit down half the time. Lizzie was no longer baffled at Juliette's laissez fare attitude, perhaps there was some truth in what she told them the night before.

Roberto gathered the cast. He clapped his hands and said in his dribbly voice, 'you have a twenty-minute break. Prepare yourself we are doing a new number, a Russian Can-Can'.

The cast looked at each other, eyebrows raising. One of the new girls, Tracy, piped up: 'That's against the rules, we're supposed to have at least a 6-hour break before we perform.'

Amelia turned and told her sarcastically: 'There are no Equity rules here, honey, Have you seen your contract since Mexico?'

The rehearsal went on for more than two hours. The opening ten minutes in the number consisted of dancing around the rickety stage using Cossack formations in figures of eight, doing kicks and squats. Roberto made the cast do it over and over again, shouting at the dancers, spit flying everywhere. Everybody cursed him under their breath. This was followed by a Can-Can kick line, and split jumps with combinations of high kicks. Everyone stood in a line, the tallest in the centre and the shortest fanning out to either side. Hands across each other's shoulders. They had to do sixteen high kicks in exact timing starting from the two girls in the centre, in an outward formation. Every time somebody missed a beat, they had to start again.

"It was Juliette." snitched Amelia.

Karen shouted at Juliette to get her shit together. Lizzie could see the smirk in Roberto's face. It was clear he was enjoying himself. Lizzie had always known he had a mean streak. But she couldn't believe that he was doing it to punish them. At the sixth attempt, Lizzie stepped forward and said to Roberto: "I'm not doing it anymore." Everyone turned and looked at her, mouths open. Lizzie said:

"My hamstrings are going to pop!"

Maya repeated it to Roberto, with disdain. Roberto just turned round with a smirk and walks off, his hen boy scurrying after him. The cast remained on the stage, looking baffled.

After a few minutes, Roberto flounced back on stage. He told the rest of the cast to rest on the side of the stage, they were only too glad to have a rest and get a sip of water.

Roberto decided to introduce some partner work with the three male members, Jason, Brian and Matias. Jason's partner was Maya, but he couldn't lift her, struggling to remove Maya's fat thighs from his face as he tried to do a Russian spin with her.

For a moment, Lizzie forgot about the pain in her hamstrings, trying to stifle her laugh at the comical sight of the partner dance. It was both funny and painful to watch. Lizzie wondered how they were going to perform it. Perhaps Roberto had the same thoughts as he ended the rehearsal abruptly. He clapped his hands dramatically and announced: "That's enough! Vamos!"

As she watched him leave, Lizzie had a quiet disdain for him. She had lost her respect for him, especially after seeing the despicable ways he treated, or mistreated, his assistant. He was absolutely vile to the young boy, treating him like a slave. Shouting at him, kicking him for not lighting his cigarette quickly enough. Lizzie often wondered why would a boy as young as him be working for someone like Roberto, where were his parents?

The dancers were the geese laying the golden eggs; it was not easy to recruit English dancers; they were well protected as long as they were under the Equity contract.

After the gruelling rehearsal, the cast went back to the apartment while the newcomers had to go for a costume fitting. But before the old cast members left, they were told the next day they had to come back two hours earlier for the new Can-Can costume fitting. Lizzie didn't mind, she had already taken a peek at the new costume when she went to say hello to Alba, the costume lady. She was really happy she wouldn't be fitted in a slutty costume but would instead be in a sweet Cossack costume in red, boots, fur pillar box hat, and neck and bottom trimmed with black fur. Her only concern was that they had to carry little flags with them.

Lizzie, Karen, and Ellie went into the trailer. Tammy was in there crying. She had been told she could go home when the new girls arrived. She could not wait to go back to see her parents. The girls tried to console her, Tammy just sobbed, saying "you don't understand" repeatedly. Lizzie looked across, and Olivia and Lorraine were sitting there. They both looked incredibly sad, looking as though they were crying but yet not crying.

Gustavo appeared with the Smooth Operator, and the company was told that even though some members have their own accommodation, they were to keep to the strict rules and make sure that they arrived in good time for the performances, and that they would only be remaining in Costa Rica for two weeks before moving on to Panama. This came as quite a shock to Lizzie, never has the cast been informed at such an early stage about future tour dates. After announcing the itinerary, Gustavo departed abruptly.

That night the cast left earlier than usual for the circus because they had to do a pre-show stage rehearsal as the new cast needed to be introduced to their roles. Nobody spoke a word, as if in unwritten consensus, about what they had been told. They did not even discuss this amongst themselves, it was as though they either could not believe the enormity of it, or the thought that they might be thrown into jail. While the whole cast waited for Roberto's arrival, the air felt rather different. The normal excitement at rehearsals was missing. Dancers did not even bother to warm up, they were just slouching around. Lizzie saw Tammy sitting at the far side of the stage. She was crying. Her boyfriend, one of the Mexican circus hands, was trying to comfort her. She pushed him away. News always travelled fast in the circus. It was soon known to everyone that Tammy was not allowed to go home to see her family in Iowa, and she had been waiting for more than two years to leave.

Roberto appeared out of nowhere, like a spectre. Standing next to him was his long-time and trusted assistant Pedro, who was looking quite worse for wear, as if he has been dragged backward through a hedge. He looked deeply sorry for himself, standing demurely next to Roberto. Roberto clapped his hands loudly. Rehearsals began and the new cast members were placed in their position for the opening number. For some reason, Juliette, who had recently implied that the circus was not really what it was and filling the cast members' heads with stories of illegal shenanigans, was starting to irritate Roberto. Roberto shouted at her repeatedly, getting louder and more irritated:

"Step-ball-change! Step-ball-change!"

Quite unusual for Roberto, he started to demonstrate the steps, but it was really comical to the cast, as he looked like a puppet on a string with his anorexic body. It looked like the strings, if they were there, would not even hold him up. He was looking like a marionette completely out of control. Roberto's focus shifted away from Juliette when he realized that most of the dancers were laughing at him. Like a flick of a switch, his demeanour changed, and he then insisted that all the cast members repeat the dance move endlessly. Lizzie was already suffering shin splints from having to dance on an unsprung metal floor for seven months. Now her knees were really hurting. It felt like an eternity before Roberto clapped his hands and ended the rehearsal. There was no time for any break or refreshments. The cast members went straight to the trailers to prepare for the evening show.

Just before curtains up, Tammy burst into the trailer. She had returned from seeing Gustavo. She was smiling like a Cheshire cat who got the cream. She announced excitedly that she was going home; Gustavo was going to pay for it and she would be going via Miami as she had been tasked with taking an urgent parcel with her. She was thrilled to be able to stay an extra week in Miami, all expenses paid. Lizzie could see from the side of her eyes that Olivia looked concerned at Tammy's announcement. But nobody said anything as they did not want to burst Tammy's bubbles. They clapped and congratulated her. Lizzie thought to herself:

"There is something not right here."

Little did Lizzie know that that night was going to be her last show. The performance that night was the best the cast had done. Everyone, including the audience was enthralled by the performance.

Lizzie, Karen, Susan and Ellie's taxi was delayed picking them up from the circus. Ellie, Susan, and Karen slunk off to have a cigarette. Lizzie stayed to wait for the taxi. Feeling a little chilly, she paced around, rubbing her forearms vigorously. Lizzie looked around and saw the Smooth Operator had Olivia pinned to a wall, trying to force a kiss on her. Lizzie could hear Olivia shouting, trying to push him away. He grabbed her by the hair and pulled her back to him, slapping her twice around the face. Lizzie stood there, frozen with fear. She wanted to try and do something to help but she just could not move. She was sure that Olivia could see her as the latter was turned toward her. Lizzie was sure that Olivia was shaking her head slightly, as if to warn Lizzie not to come over. Lizzie could see that he was more violent to Olivia and forced himself on her. At that point, Lizzie heard Karen calling out to her that the taxi has arrived, and she turned and ran toward the girls. In the taxi, Lizzie's thoughts were in turmoil as she could not understand why Olivia would allow a man to do that to her, and why she stayed there. She was thinking Olivia must have been on an Equity contract, surely, and she should therefore be legally protected under those contractual conditions and allowed to leave when she wants. She wished she had gone over to save her. At that time, she did not realize that she would not see Olivia again. That last images of the violence Olivia had experienced was ingrained in her mind for a long time after. Her thoughts were interrupted by Jason babbling on that the latest gossip was that the circus was in trouble. There was no money because they were stopped at the borders of Nicaragua entering into Costa Rica, and that drugs had been seized, hence there was a delay in the performance schedule.

Back at the apartment, there was a visit by one of Gustavo's security men. Lizzie was informed that in the morning, she was going to be leaving for London. Nobody else was told that, only Lizzie. She rushed to her room to get her diary out. The next morning would have been the last day of her seventh month contract. She was ecstatic! She was overjoyed that the craziness and the hardship of the last seven months would be coming to an end.

CHAPTER 5

Going Home

It took ages for Lizzie to pack. No one in the cast could believe she was going. Next morning, a knock on the door came. It was the same security man. Karen was awake, she was crying, upset to see Lizzie leaving. No one else was up yet. Lizzie said goodbye to Karen, gave her a big hug and got into the taxi waiting outside the apartment. At that moment, she was a little sad and felt that she would definitely miss everyone in the cast. After all, they had spent seven months together, going through the craziest of adventures.

The journey to the airport took ages. At one point, Lizzie started wondering if she was really going to the airport or was being taken elsewhere. She tried to ask the taxi driver, but he just said nothing and smoked away. Getting nowhere, Lizzie tried to settle back onto the seat, but the thoughts in her brain would not quieten. On the one hand, she was relieved to be going home, but on the other, she could not help wondering:

"Why am I being sent home on the very last day of my seventh month contract, even though there was a clause in the contract that a dancer could be kept for another four weeks in case there were delays in the new girl coming?"

As the question flit through her mind, she began to start panicking. Looking out of the car window, it was just a vast, empty landscape and there were no other cars on the road. She began to wonder if she was really being taken to the airport. Her thoughts flew back to the scene in the trailer – perhaps Gustavo had not done a deal and she was being taken to the shit circus after all. In a panic, she tried to use her limited Spanish and asked the driver again:

"Signor, donde es a'lerporto?"

He ignored her but she kept badgering him until he finally replied:

"One hour and 10 minutes."

After that there was complete silence between them for the rest of the journey. Occasionally, Lizzie's eyes met his via his rear-view mirror. He drove like a maniac down the hot and dusty and deserted route. Lizzie asked to stop to go to the toilet once and he simply kept saying "non". He just rattled along as though his life depended on him getting her to the airport. Eventually, Lizzie drifted off to sleep after convincing herself that she was indeed going to the airport.

After what seemed like eternity, they arrived. The car screeched to a halt and Lizzie was jolted from her sleep. She got out in a daze. It did not look like an airport. It was only an air strip with one small, dinky office. Just one person was in there. The check-in man informed Lizzie that she could not get on the flight as she had not paid her airport tax. She went back outside to speak to the driver who was still there, leaning by his car smoking his cigarette. He did not understand her, of course.

Just as Lizzie was wondering what to do, a car came

speeding along the dirt track, sending a cloud of dust up in the air. It stopped with a screech, and lo and behold, Gustavo got out. He did not look his usual immaculate self. He was hot and sweaty, standing before Lizzie, with his huge belly hanging over his trousers, as though he had to leave in a hurry.

The check-in man came out to tell Lizzie that if she was to fly, she would have to pay her airport tax and board soon. At that point, Gustavo said to Lizzie, all the airport taxes will be paid. He added that somebody at Mexico City will pay the airport tax when she arrives there. Gustavo was standing there, with his somewhat crumpled Italian shirt, unruly beard, big Stetson hat, chewing on his cigar. Lizzie could not help wonder why he had come all the way to pay for her airport tax. He stepped forward and offered his hand to Lizzie. Lizzie hesitated and did not shake his hand. She was afraid Gustavo was going to drag her back to his car. she wanted to but it was like time stood still, and in the end, she did not shake his hands. Before she could get her head around what had happened, Gustavo turned and left, just as swiftly as he appeared. She was then told to get on the tiny, propeller plane. It took her to Mexico City airport.

Disembarking from the tiny plane, Lizzie was greeted by a well-spoken man who took her to the check-in desk. She almost made it on to the flight to Huston, Texas, as there was still time to spare. But then the check-in girl said:

"This is an open return ticket, you need to return on the same journey as the one you had come out on."

That meant that she had to go to Monterrey to take her flight. She was put on the last flight to Monterrey, with mainly Mexicans on the plane. Upon arrival, the Mexicans just scuttled away, leaving Lizzie on her own in the deserted airport. All she could see were some male cleaners who had just arrived. They looked at her snidely. Lizzie felt really uncomfortable. She was too afraid to get out of her seat to even go to the toilet.

Suddenly, a well-dressed man showed up in front of her. He told Lizzie that there was no flight to Huston until tomorrow morning. He told her that she should not stay there on her own. Glancing over at those men still staring at Lizzie, he said quite bluntly that she would be raped by those men. Tears rolled down Lizzie's eyes, her lips trembled. He took pity on her and took her to his office. He looked at her passport and ticket. He then checked Lizzie in for the first flight out. He joked that it was meant to be that they met. If it were his colleague, he would not have prioritized Lizzie on the flight. He said his colleague did not like Americans. Lizzie said she is not American but English. He said:

"It did not matter, you are not Mexican."

He turned round and asked Lizzie if she would like to join him as he was about to go off duty and get something to eat. Lizzie was slightly taken aback. She chewed her lips and thought about this, weighing her choices:

"Shall I stay at the airport and possibly be raped by the cleaners, or take the chances and go with him?"

If necessary, she could handle one man but not two. In her mind she was thinking she might just get away with giving him a hand job.

She got in his car. He introduced himself as Alejandro. They drove towards the mountains. He said in a softly spoken voice:

"I'm going to show you something magical. Don't be frightened, I am not going to hurt you."

Inside, Lizzie was petrified but she tried her utmost not to show her trepidation. Finally, they got to the top of the mountain. Alejandro parked the car, took out 2 bottles of Sprite from the back of his car, ushering Lizzie out of his car. He told her to turn around. Lizzie turned around and before her, millions of tiny lights like lanterns flickered away. It was the city of Monterrey. Lizzie felt like she was looking down from heaven. The night sky was filled with stars. She started to relax a little. They chatted away. Lizzie told Alejandro about her dancing in the circus and where they had been. Alejandro spoke about his wife and two children. Then he drove her down the mountain again, and they arrived at an eatery. It had a saloon-type door. Lizzie needed to go to the toilet, it was disgusting but she had no other choice. He then ordered tortillas. Lizzie gobbled it up, not caring about her usual reticence of eating hot spicy food. Alejandro paid for the meal and drove her back to the airport. The sun was starting to rise. He gave Lizzie her case, her ticket and passport. Lizzie returned to the same spot he had found her. He said to Lizzie he had to go back to his duty but will come and say goodbye later. He did just that, saw Lizzie to the airplane, and Lizzie was finally on the flight to Huston, safe and sound.

From the softness and kindness of Alejandro in Mexico City, Lizzie was greeted by a harsh and loud-voiced check-in receptionist at Huston airport, basically telling her that she could not board the flight for London Heathrow as her ticket was an off-peak one. She would be booked in for the late 11 pm flight. Lizzie found herself having to spend eleven hours at Huston airport. She looked around, at least this looked more like a normal airport and there were plenty of passengers around. With hardly any money on her, exhausted from not having slept a wink last night, she looked around and see a security man looking at her. She thought to herself:

"At least this looked more like a normal airport, and there are plenty of passengers around."

She went to the toilet, got some paper towels, found some toothpaste in her holdall, brushed her teeth and cleaned herself as much as she could. She got back to the lounge, spending many hours people watching. Finally, she boarded the flight. At this point, she no longer cared where she would be seated on the airplane. Fortunately, she was given a window seat with an empty seat next to hers. There was no delay to the departure and the plane's engine revved up, the powerful engine sounds booming as it taxied the runway. Soon they were airborne. Lizzie felt drained and was absolutely starving as she had not eaten nor drunk anything since the kindly Alejandro fed her at the dingy little diner. She had never been so happy to hear the voice of the air stewardess asking her what she wanted for her meal. She was not fussed about it, and just wolfed down her food and the watery cup of tea. She settled down as the plane sailed through the night sky. She was utterly exhausted, yet she could not sleep, her mind turning toward the matter of getting a refund for all the horrible experience she had in Mexico and the prospect of getting her Equity card. She decided she would have as good night's sleep at her mum's, get up early the next morning and go to the Equity Office. She would confront the Head of Equity and demand to have a refund of her £50s as she had injured her knees performing in the circus in Mexico. She could do with the money to get her knees seen to. She made up her mind there and then that she was going to stay at the Office and not leave until she got her Equity card.

A rustling of paper made her open her eyes. She looked up and the man in the seat in front of her had his papers spread out. She saw in the headlines:

"UK Equity Scandal: Bribery and corruption!"

Lizzie was shocked! She thought:

"What is this about? Is this a coincidence?"

She tapped the man on the shoulder and asked if she could read the paper when he was finished with it. He shrugged and passed it to her. Lizzie waded through the article and as she was reading, she started to realize that in fact she was reading about her very own experience of Equity contract. She realized that the events over the past seven months were no coincidence. The puzzles that she had in her mind throughout those times began to fall into place and the terrifying reality hit her that she could have been stopped from returning home. Thinking back to Gustavo appearing out of the blue at the airport to see her off and to ensure that the airport taxes were paid in Costa Rica and also at Mexico City, Lizzie began to wonder if Gustavo was in fact her protector, and he wanted to personally make sure that she left safely. She felt a slight twinge of regret as she thought:

"Maybe I should have shaken his hands after all."

Only he would have known what the alternative would have been for Lizzie had she not left. All clues led to a criminal incentive under the disguise of a glamourous travelling circus show. She was somehow dragged into this world of deceit and sinister operation that was happening behind the scenes. Lizzie could not believe how naive and uneducated she was in the ways of the world.

As her mind eventually turned away from the Equity matter, she began to drift into sleep from sheer exhaustion. But before dropping off, she thought about the fact that even though the country was so poor, they were never far away from a good coffee place. She began to think that it might be a good idea to start a coffee house in London, which had no good cafés around that served great milky coffee. The thought excited Lizzie, but it was soon diminished when she remembered the papers were still reporting on the Black Monday stock market crash. Who would give a working class girl like her someone any credit to follow a new business dream?

Upon landing at Heathrow airport, Lizzie breezed through passport control. She finally breathed a sigh of relief, she had arrived home safely. She dragged her luggage on to the train and headed back to her mum's house. Lizzie had had no time to let her family know of her return. Feeling excited as she let herself in, the feeling quickly ebbed away as she shut the door behind her, and she could smell an ominous atmosphere. It filled her with dread. She brushed the thought away, as she turned to the thought of going to London first thing next day to the Equity Office to demand the Equity card that she had rightfully earned. It was the passport to her dreams of living the life as a professional dancer.